GOLDY'S BABY SOCKS

By Judy Snider

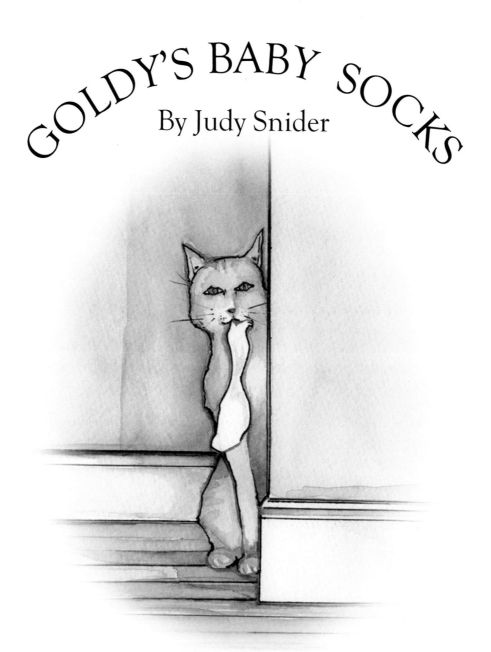

Illustrated By Thomas McAteer

To: Gil, my husband, and my sons, Jon and Nick-I love you,
  You are wonderful! Thanks for helping make a dream come true.

To: Mom, Dad, Mary, Joan, Fred, Michael, Tracy and Christy-My
  Michigan Family...
  I love y'all.

ACKNOWLEDGEMENTS

Lots of people made this book possible:

My thanks to:

My wonderful friends who are also all my co-workers at Cape Henry Collegiate Library-my family away from home.

My Cape Henry Collegiate Writer's Group Friends.

The TERRIFIC kids I read to at Cape Henry Collegiate and the kind staff/faculty there.

Lindsay, Zena, Nancy M., Nancy L., Linda, Ellen, Eleanor, Karen, Kathy, Cindy, Sylvia, Sarah, Dot, Bev, Jo, Mary Ellen, and David M.—Thanks for listening to my dreams of publishing a book.

Joel, Josh and Liana Snider

Steely and Tony

Many thanks to the wonderful illustrator of this book, Thomas McAteer, who makes the story come alive with his drawings.

Ariel, Mary and the rest of he team at Xlibris who guided me through the publishing process.

Library of Congress Number:		2005907480
ISBN:	Softcover	978-1-5992-6453-0
	Hardcover	978-1-5992-6454-7

Print information available on the last page.

To order additional copies of this book, contact:
Xlibris
1-888-795-4274
www.Xlibris.com
Orders@Xlibris.com

We have a cat that lives with us. SHE'S the reason that we almost had to move out of our house.

Goldy was a stray cat that came to us one beautiful summer morning. She was skinny, had huge green eyes, and was a shiny gold color. We decided to call her Goldy. No one claimed her, so we kept her.

It was no time before Goldy was sleeping on my parent's bed. That's when all the WEIRD stuff began.

One night, Goldy quickly jumped off the bed. After awhile we heard a soft noise coming down the hall.
"Mew . . . mew . . . purrrrrr . . .
Mew . . . . Mew . . ."

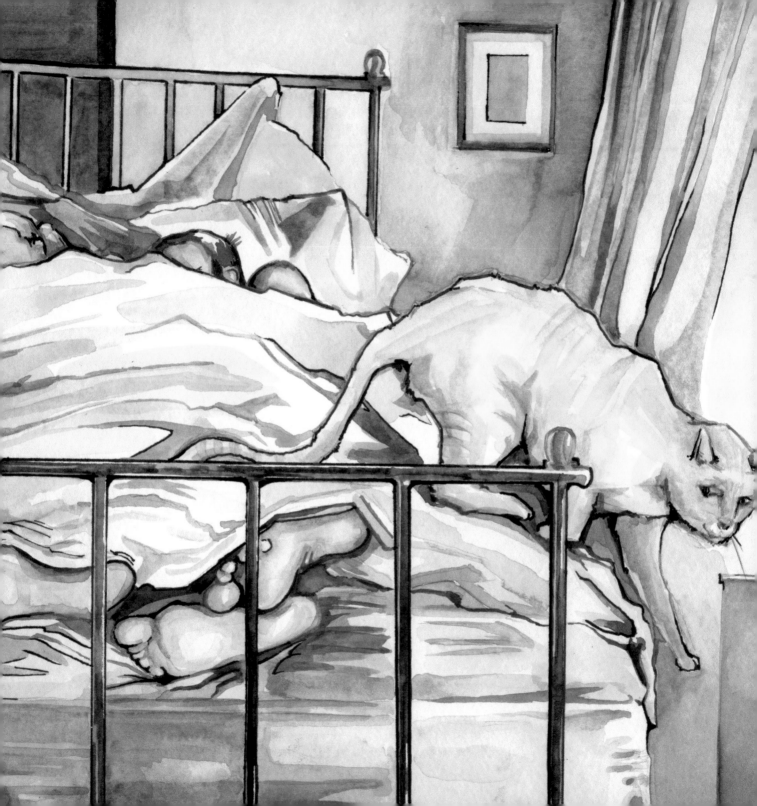

We jumped out of bed to see what was wrong. There was Goldy wobbling down the hall, softly mewing with a sock hanging from her mouth.

"Mew . . . Mew" Goldy said as she brought the sock to Mom and Dad's bedroom and dropped it on the floor. Goldy licked the sock over and over.

My brother and I thought it was
WEIRD, but Mom thought it was cute.
"Oh, look, Goldy's brought us her baby!"
"That's not a baby," we said. "It's just a
dumb old sock."
"Oh no, look how she carried it," Mom
laughed. "Just like cats carry their kittens."
We thought Mom was teasing us,
but she wasn't.

Goldy started meowing down the hall every night and brought us her socks. One night, Goldy dropped two socks. "Oh Goldy, you've brought us your babies," Mom chuckled, her eyes dancing with delight.

Soon Goldy brought us three, then four socks. One night, we decided to put the basket of socks away, so she couldn't get to them. All of a sudden, she walked down the hall and dropped my Dad's underwear on the floor!

"BABY UNDERWEAR!" we yelled as we rolled on the floor laughing.

"You're going to hurt Goldy's feelings if you make fun of her," Mom said, smiling, as she reached down to pick her up and cuddle her. We thought that was the end of that, but . . .

The next day, Goldy brought us five socks.
. . . Then six socks
. . . Then seven socks
. . . Then ten socks.
There were so many socks all over when we
woke up, that we had to watch
where we stepped.

Soon there were piles of socks so big I could dive into them. I even had to put on my goggles and snorkel and swim through the big piles of socks just to find my shoes!
The piles just got bigger
. . . And bigger
. . . And BIGGER!
Now Mom was beginning to think maybe we DID have a problem!

That weekend we got SO sick of cleaning up socks that we took a trip to Grandma and Grandpa's.

We told Grandma and Grandpa our Goldy story and they laughed especially at the part about Dad's UNDERWEAR. It was so great not to have to pick up socks, but soon we began to miss Goldy.

"I hope your cat hasn't done any more mischief," Grandma said that evening.

Mom got real quiet all of a sudden and said, "I have a feeling something has happened to Goldy. Let's go back tomorrow."

Mom usually doesn't panic, but something in her voice worried my brother and me. We tossed and turned all night.

We all got up early the next day, kissed our grandparents goodbye, and headed home. When we drove up our driveway, Mom screamed, "I CAN'T SEE IN THE WINDOWS! THEY'RE BLOCKED BY SOCKS!"
We all ran to the door and unlocked it. Out poured socks, underwear, towels, and shirts on the steps.

"Oh no!" we cried, making a path to get inside of the house. "We must find Goldy!"
. . . We made our way through the clothes to the kitchen, but we couldn't find Goldy.
. . . We made our way to the living room, but we couldn't find Goldy.
. . . We made our way to the bathroom, but we couldn't find Goldy.
Finally, we climbed through the socks in the hallway and made our way to the bedroom.

There, sitting on top of a two-foot pile of socks was Goldy, surrounded by two tiny kittens, smiling and looking Oh-so proud! We all laughed and patted her gently on her head. We did not touch the kittens as they were too tiny, but we all sat by them and told Goldy she sure was a good mother.

She must have been practicing how to carry her kittens in her mouth by using socks. She seemed to understand we thought she was terrific and meowed softly to us. We begged our parents to keep the kittens and they said, "Of course! Any baby of Goldy's is part of our family."

You know, after we cleaned up the socks, she never brought in more than one. Thank Goodness!!!

QUESTIONS FOR CHILDREN

1. Do you have a pet in your home?
2. What kind of pet do you have?
3. What is your pet's Name?

Printed in the United States
By Bookmasters